JUV/E8
FIC
HALL

EASTSI

D1468551

CHICAGO PUBLIC LIBRARY
VODAK EASTSIDE BRANCH
3710 EAST 106 STREET
CHICAGO, IL 60617

What a Mess!

ALL ABOUT NUMBERS

Written by Kirsten Hall
Illustrated by Bev Luedecke

children's press®

A Division of Scholastic Inc.
New York   Toronto   London   Auckland   Sydney
Mexico City   New Delhi   Hong Kong
Danbury, Connecticut

About the Author

Kirsten Hall, formerly an early-childhood teacher,
is a children's book editor in New York City. She has been
writing books for children since she was thirteen years old
and now has over sixty titles in print.

About the Illustrator

Bev Luedecke enjoys life and nature in Colorado.
Her sparkling personality and artistic flair are reflected in her
creation of Beastieville, a world filled with lovable Beasties
that are sure to delight children of all ages.

Library of Congress Cataloging-in-Publication Data

Hall, Kirsten.
  What a mess! : all about numbers / written by Kirsten Hall ; illustrated by Bev Luedecke.
    p. cm. — (Beastieville)
  Summary: Toggles helps Bee-Bop clean out his house and sell the extra things he does not need.
  ISBN 0-516-23670-9 (lib. bdg.)   0-516-25524-X (pbk.)
  [1. Belongings, Personal—Fiction. 2. Orderliness—Fiction. 3. Garage sales—Fiction. 4. Stories in rhyme.]
  I. Luedecke, Bev, ill. II. Title.
  PZ8.3.H146Wf 2004
  [E]—dc22

                                             2004000130

Text © 2004 Nancy Hall, Inc. Illustrations © 2004 Bev Luedecke. All rights reserved.
Published in 2004 by Children's Press, an imprint of Scholastic Library Publishing.
Printed in the United States of America. Developed by Nancy Hall, Inc.

CHILDREN'S PRESS and associated logos are trademarks and or registered trademarks of Scholastic Library
Publishing. SCHOLASTIC and associated logos are trademarks and or registered trademarks of Scholastic Inc.

1 2 3 4 5 6 7 8 9 10 R 13 12 11 10 09 08 07 06 05 04

EAS

A NOTE TO PARENTS AND TEACHERS

Welcome to the world of the Beasties, where learning is FUN. In each of the charming stories in this series, the Beasties deal with character traits that every child can identify with. Each story reinforces appropriate concept skills for kindergartners and first graders, while simultaneously encouraging problem-solving skills. Following are just a few of the ways that you can help children get the most from this delightful series.

Stories to be read and enjoyed
Encourage children to read the stories aloud. The rhyming verses make them fun to read. Then ask them to think about alternate solutions to some of the problems that the Beasties have faced or to imagine alternative endings. Invite children to think about what they would have done if they were in the story and to recall similar things that have happened to them.

Activities reinforce the learning experience
The activities at the end of the books offer a way for children to put their new skills to work. They complement the story and are designed to help children develop specific skills and build confidence. Use these activities to reinforce skills. But don't stop there. Encourage children to find ways to build on these skills during the course of the day.

Learning opportunities are everywhere
Use this book as a starting point for talking about how we use reading skills or math or social studies concepts in everyday life. When we search for a phone number in the telephone book and scan names in alphabetical order or check a list, we are using reading skills. When we keep score at a baseball game or divide a class into even-numbered teams, we are using math.

The more you can help children see that the skills they are learning in school really do have a place in everyday life, the more they will think of learning as something that is part of their lives, not as a chore to be borne. Plus you will be sending the important message that learning is fun.

Madeline Boskey Olsen, Ph.D.
Developmental Psychologist

Chicago Public Library
Vodak / East Side Branch
3710 E. 106th St.
Chicago, IL 60617

Bee-Bop

Puddles

Slider

Wilbur

Pip & Zip

Flippet

Pooky

Mr. Rigby

We're the Beasties

Smudge

Toggles

"Hi there, Toggles!" Bee-Bop waves.
"Do you want to play with me?

I just got a brand-new game.
Come inside so you can see!"

Bee-Bop opens his front door.
"Oh!" says Toggles in surprise.

It is such a mess inside.
She cannot believe her eyes!

"Bee-Bop, this is such a mess!
We must clean up right away.

You do not need all this stuff.
Cleaning this could take all day!"

"We should start in this big room.
We will play when we are done.

These five books are all the same!
Why do you need more than one?"

"Why do you need four ice skates?
All you really need are two!

No one needs to have two pairs.
You do not need both, do you?"

"You do not need eight big balls!
Why do you need all five bats?

Bee-Bop, you have just one head.
Why do you need ten blue hats?"

"You do not need all this stuff.
Do you really need two brooms?

Help me move this stuff outside.
I must sweep these messy rooms!"

Zip and Pip are walking by.
"We have always wanted these!"

Zip and Pip hold up two books.
"Bee-Bop, can we buy these please?"

Smudge walks over. "I love blue!
Can I buy one of these hats?"

"We need some of these at school!"
Mr. Rigby buys three bats.

Flippet wants to buy a raft.
"I can sit on it to float!"

Puddles gives a nice wet spray.
"I just love my brand-new boat!"

Pooky buys three jars of paint.
Slider buys himself a hat.

Everything for sale is gone.
"I am rich! Just look at that!"

Bee-Bop looks around his house.
He thanks Toggles. "This is great!

Do you want to play my game?
Toggles, it is not too late!"

WHAT A MESS!

1. How many ice skates do you think Bee-Bop needs?

2. How many brooms does Bee-Bop have?

3. How many of Bee-Bop's friends buy things from Bee-Bop?

4. How many bats does Mr. Rigby buy? Who will use them?

SOUNDS LIKE...

"Same" is a word that sounds like "game." Can you think of any other words that sound like "game"?

CLEANING UP

Cleaning up messes is always a good idea.

1. Why is it important to keep things clean?

2. When does your room get messy?

3. Why is Bee-Bop happier in the end?

WORD LIST

a	done	inside	Pip	take
all	door	is	play	ten
always	eight	it	please	than
am	everything	jars	Pooky	thanks
and	eyes	just	Puddles	that
are	five	late	raft	the
around	Flippet	look	really	there
at	float	looks	rich	these
away	for	love	Rigby	this
balls	four	me	right	three
bats	front	mess	room	to
Bee-Bop	game	messy	rooms	Toggles
believe	gives	more	sale	too
big	gone	move	same	two
blue	got	Mr.	says	up
boat	great	must	school	walking
books	hat	my	see	walks
both	hats	need	she	want
brand-new	have	needs	should	wanted
brooms	he	nice	sit	wants
buy	head	no	skates	waves
buys	help	not	Slider	we
by	her	of	Smudge	wet
can	hi	oh	so	when
cannot	himself	on	some	why
clean	his	one	spray	will
cleaning	hold	opens	start	with
come	house	outside	stuff	you
could	I	over	such	Zip
day	ice	paint	surprise	
do	in	pairs	sweep	